FROGGY PICKS A PUMPKIN

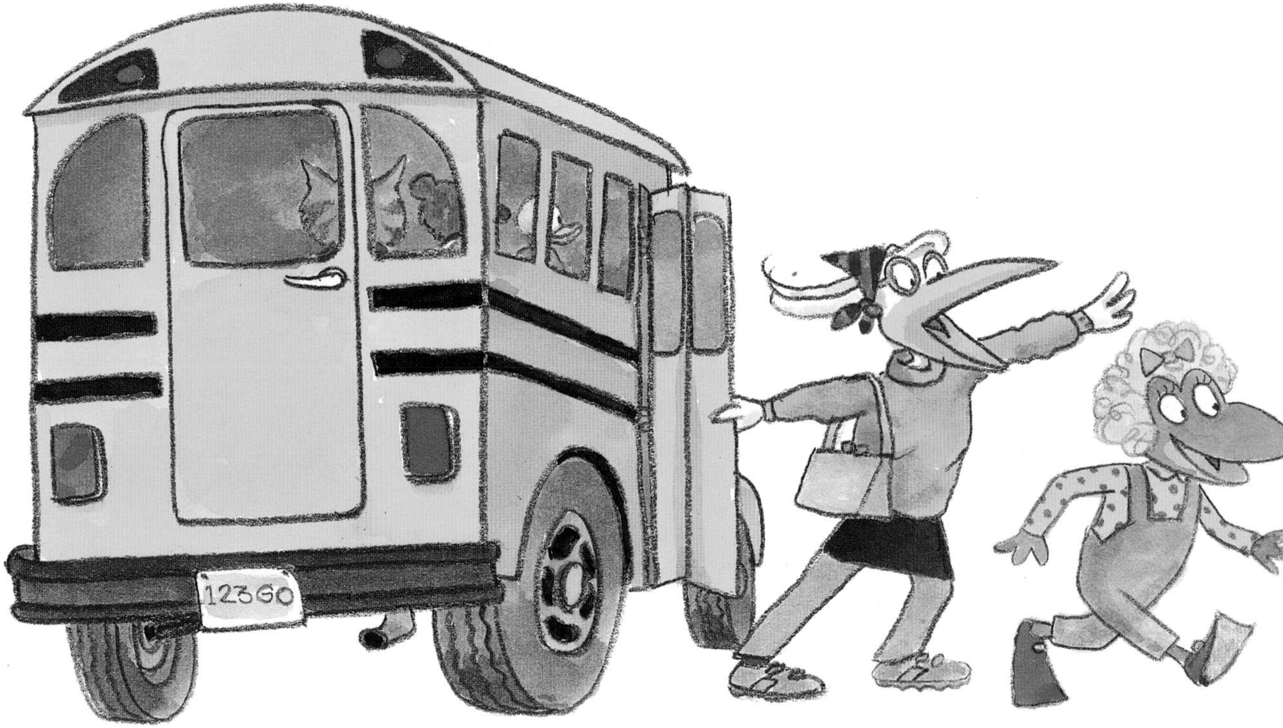
123GO

FROGGY PICKS A PUMPKIN

by JONATHAN LONDON
illustrated by FRANK REMKIEWICZ

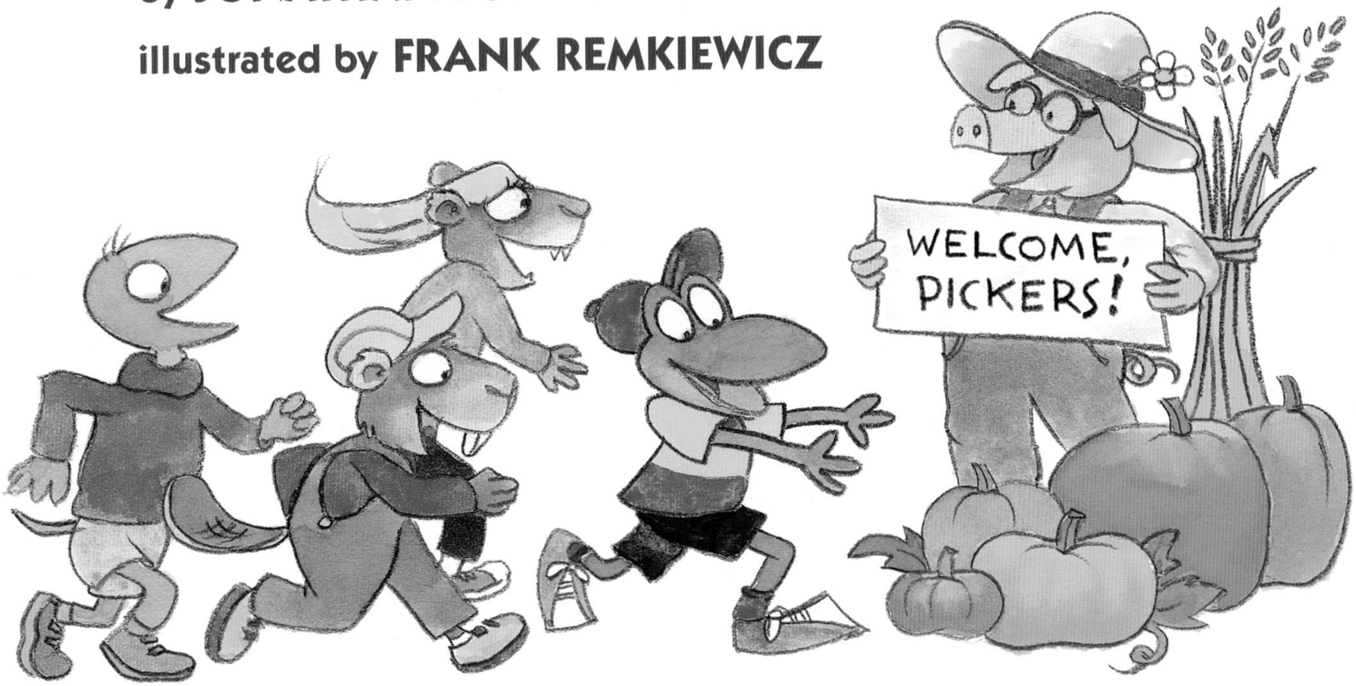
WELCOME, PICKERS!

VIKING

For Sean & Steph, Aaron, Eli, Emmett, Mikayla, Nico, Hugh,
and sweet Maureen   —J.L.

For Hannah Grace   —F.R.

VIKING
An imprint of Penguin Random House LLC
New York

First published in the United States of America by Viking, an imprint of Penguin Random House LLC, 2019

Text copyright © 2019 by Jonathan London
Illustrations copyright © 2019 by Frank Remkiewicz

Visit us online at penguinrandomhouse.com

LIBRARY OF CONGRESS CATALOGING-IN-PUBLICATION DATA IS AVAILABLE
ISBN 9781984836335

Manufactured in China   Set in ITC Kabel Std   These illustrations were made with watercolor.

10   9   8   7   6   5   4   3   2   1

At school, Froggy read a poster:

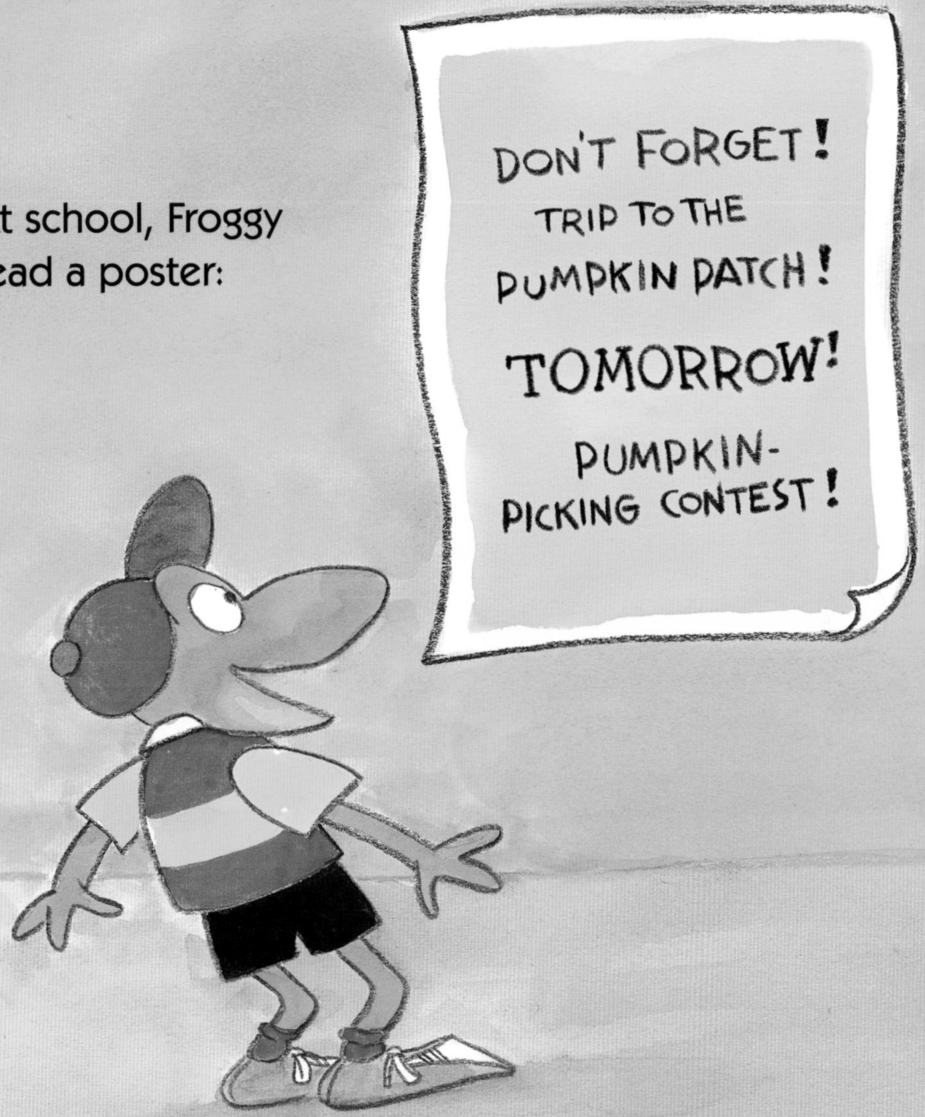
DON'T FORGET!
TRIP TO THE
PUMPKIN PATCH!
TOMORROW!
PUMPKIN-
PICKING CONTEST!

Next morning, Froggy woke up
and looked out the window.
A beautiful Pumpkin Moon
was setting and colorful leaves
were falling.

"Leaves! Leaves!" cried Froggy.
"I want to go out and play in the . . . Oops!"
He fell out of bed—

THUMP!

FRROOGGYY!

called his mother.
"Wha-a-a-a-t?"

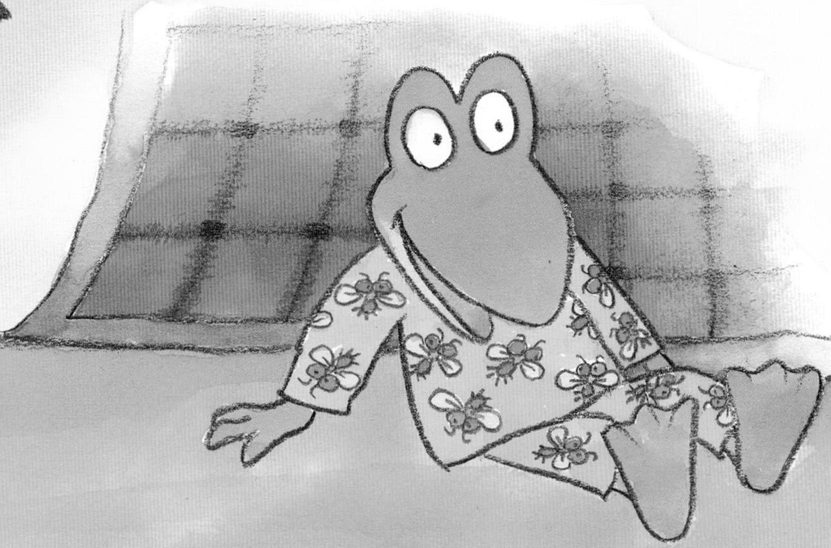

"Stop jumping off the bed, dear!
Today is your field trip!"
"Oh, yeah!" cried Froggy.
"It's time to pick a pumpkin!"

And he hopped up and got dressed—
zip! zoop! zup!
zut! zut! zut! zat!

and flopped into the kitchen—
flop flop flop—singing:

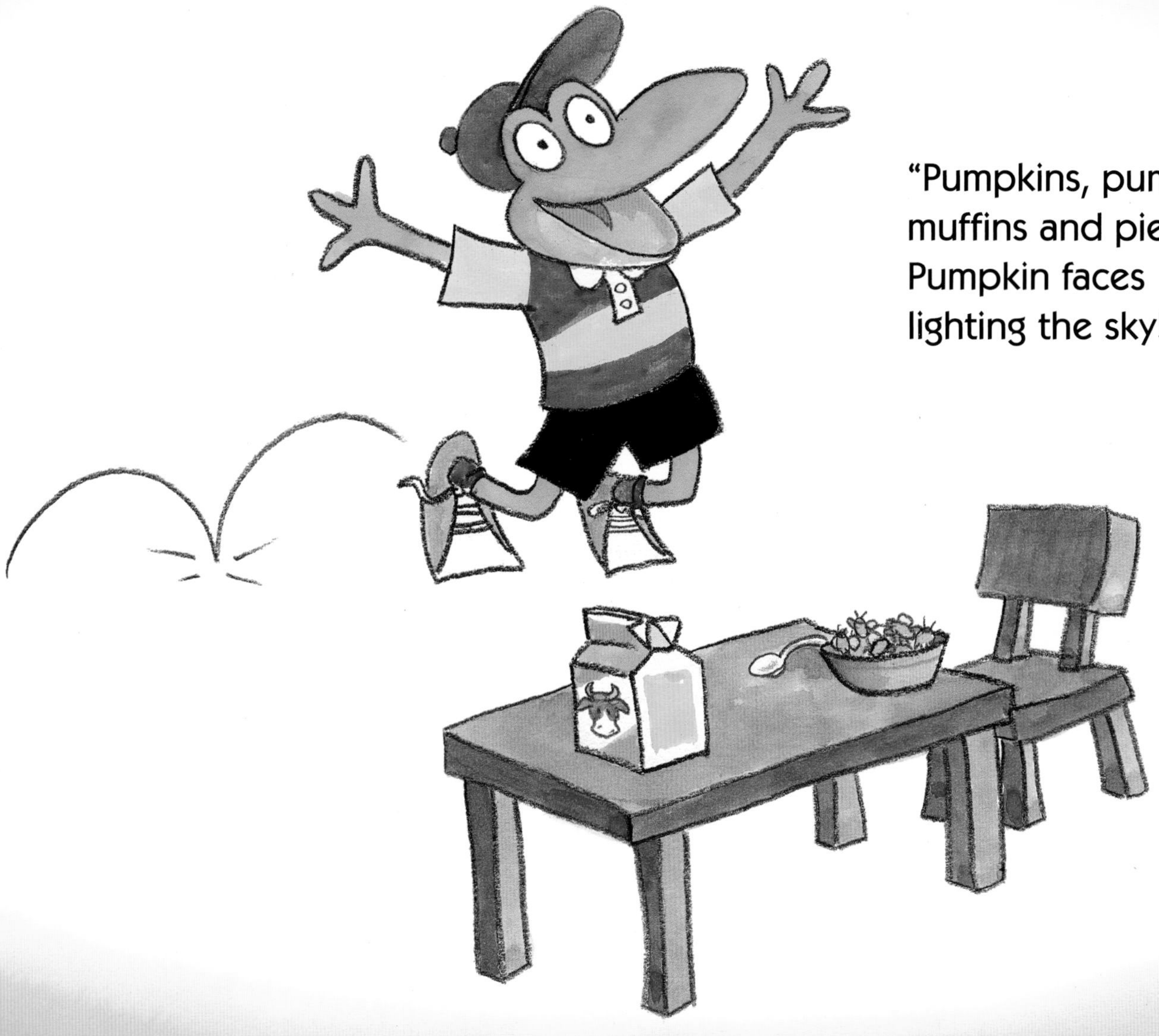

"Pumpkins, pumpkins,
muffins and pie!
Pumpkin faces
lighting the sky!"

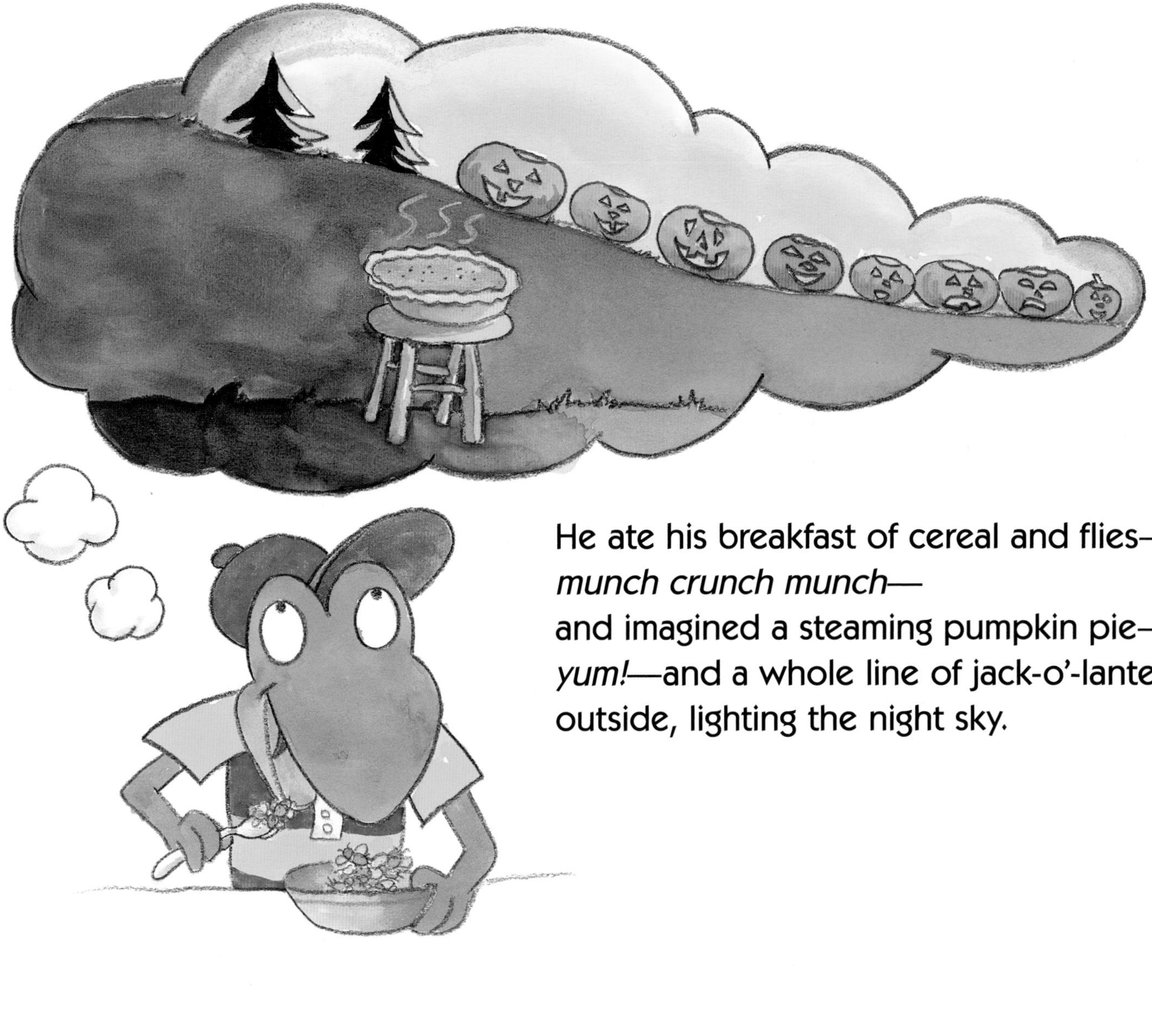

He ate his breakfast of cereal and flies—
munch crunch munch—
and imagined a steaming pumpkin pie—
yum!—and a whole line of jack-o'-lanterns
outside, lighting the night sky.

On the school bus, Froggy
bounced in his seat—
boing! boing! boing!—
and led all his friends singing:

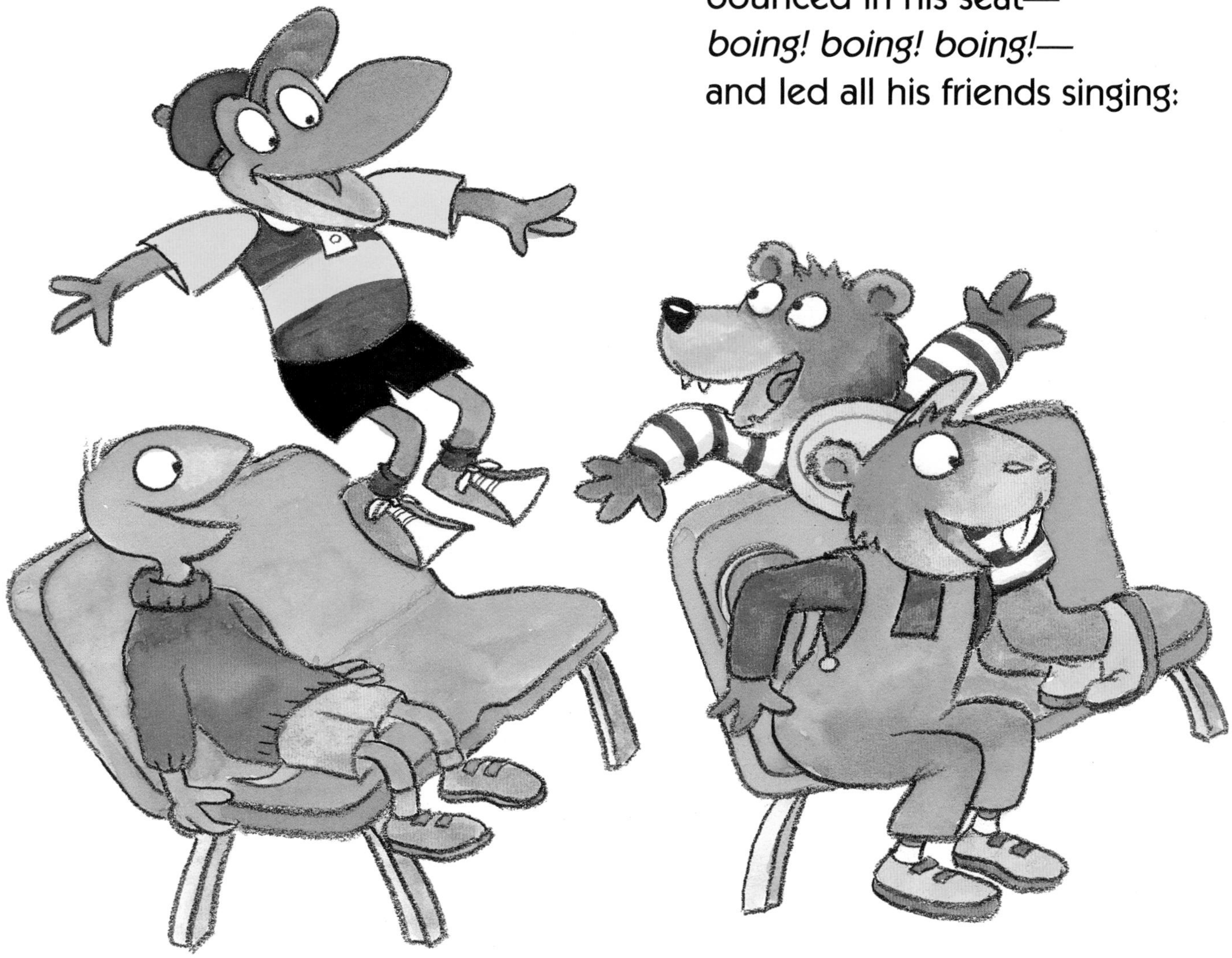

“Pumpkins, pumpkins,
muffins and pie!
Pumpkin faces
lighting the sky!”

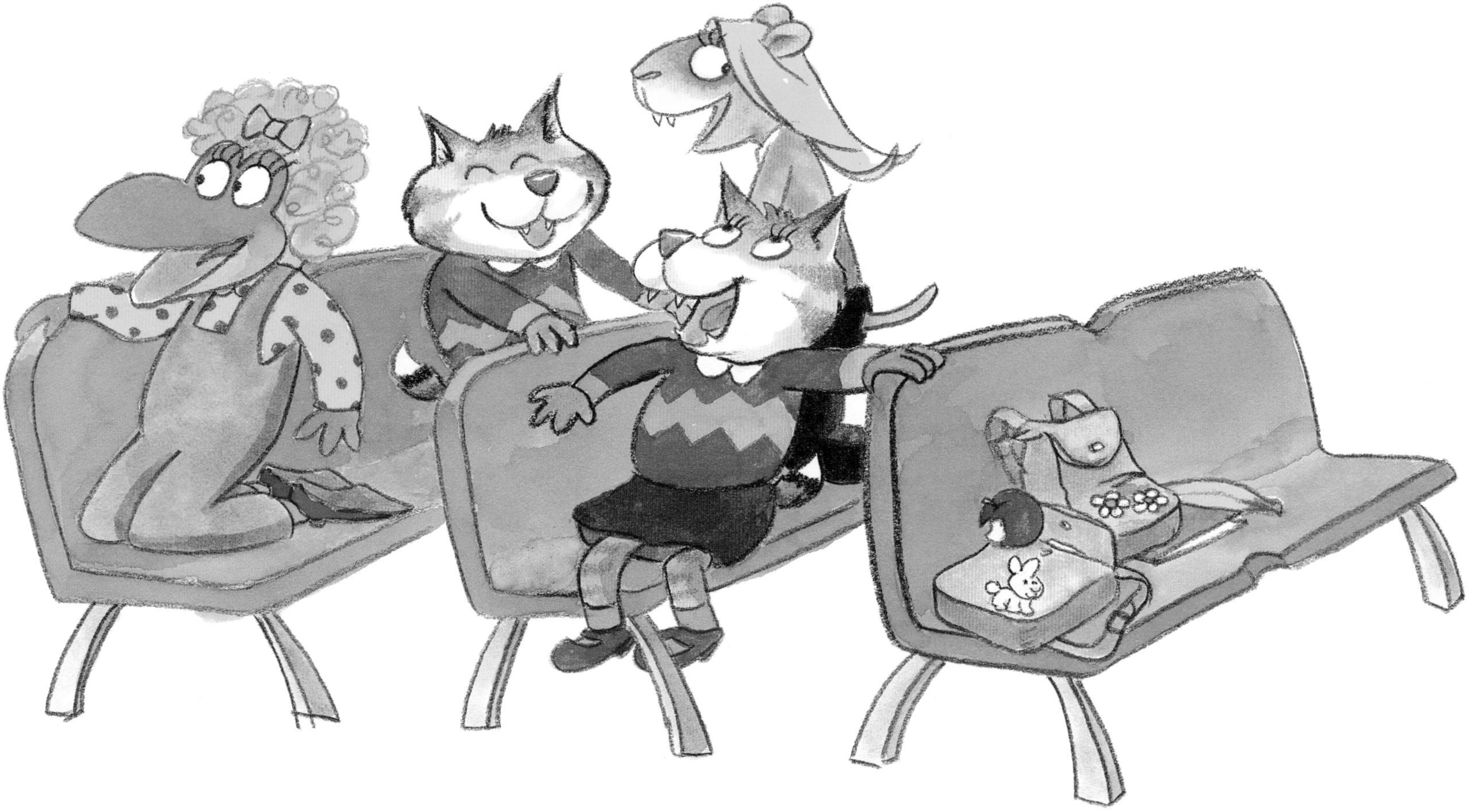

When they got to the pumpkin patch,
he jumped off the bus—*flop! flop! flop!*—
and sang, "I'm going to pick a pumpkin!
I'm going to pick a pumpkin!"

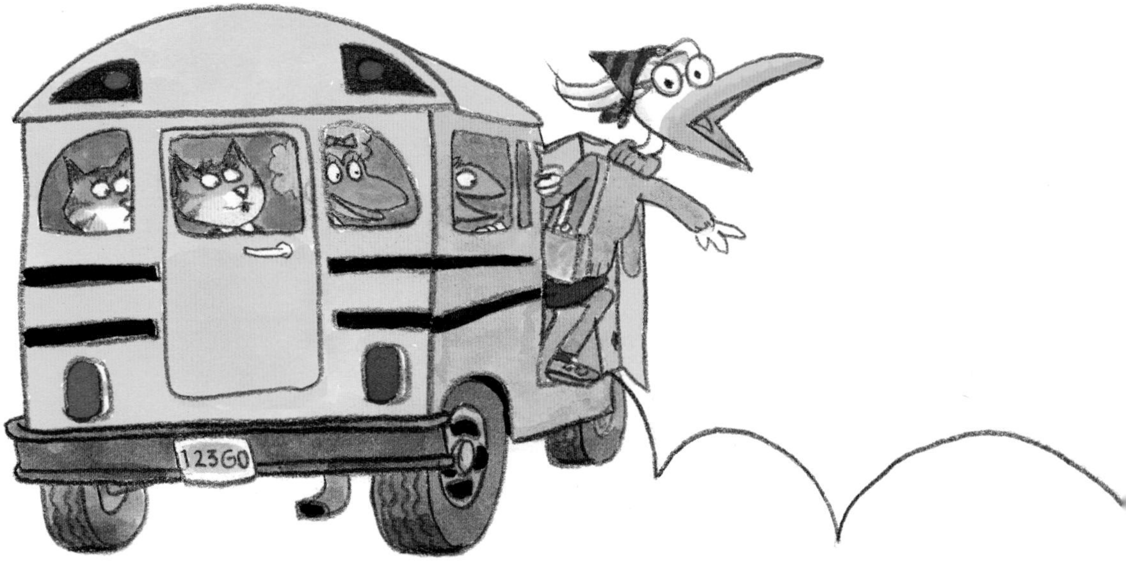
123GO

FRROOGGYY!

called his teacher, Miss Witherspoon.
"Wha-a-a-a-t?"
"Wait, dear!
We're going to have a pumpkin-
picking contest!
For the biggest, smallest, prettiest,
ugliest, and best all-around pumpkin!"

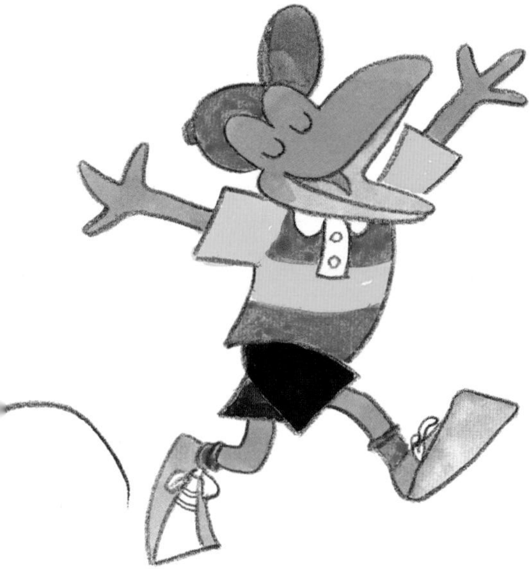

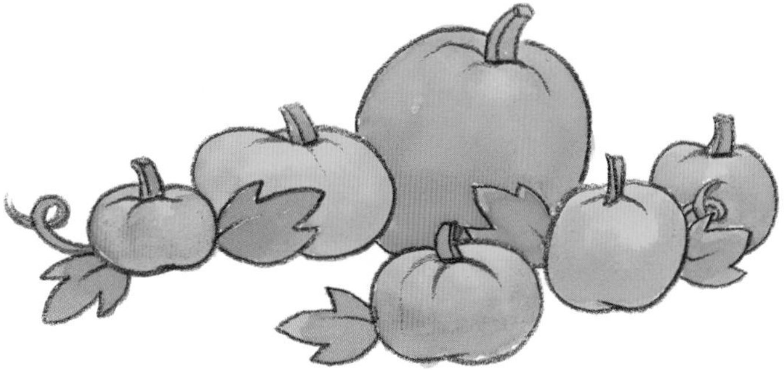

"YIPPEE!" cried Froggy, and he took
off again—*flop! flop! flop!*—
and tripped over a pumpkin . . .
flew through the air . . . and knocked
into another pumpkin—*BONK!*

Max bounced over three small pumpkins
and tried to pick up a huge one.
It didn't budge. "Ugh!"

Travis said, "Step aside!" and lifted it up!

Matthew zigzagged around Max, Travis, and Froggy,
and picked up the prettiest pumpkin in the world.
It was shiny and perfect and just the right size.

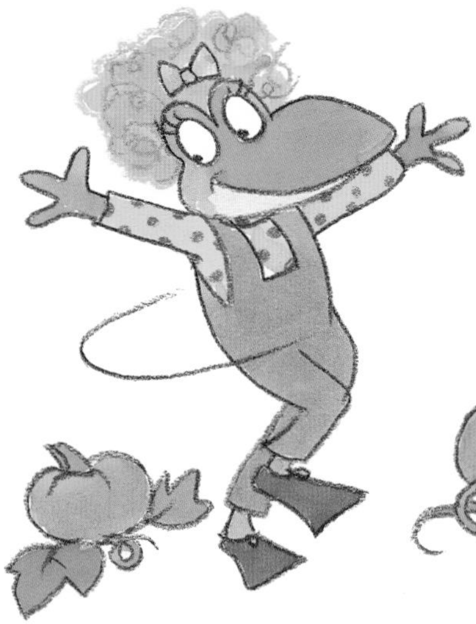

Frogilina twirled and danced
through the pumpkin patch,

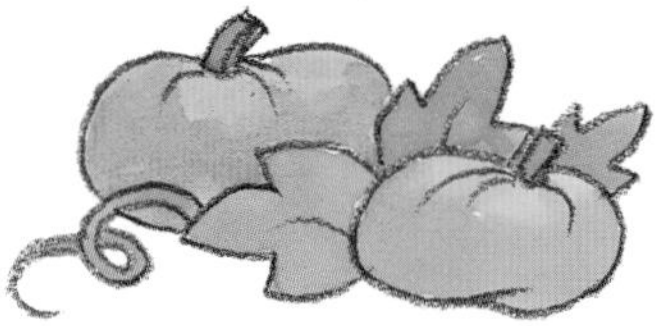

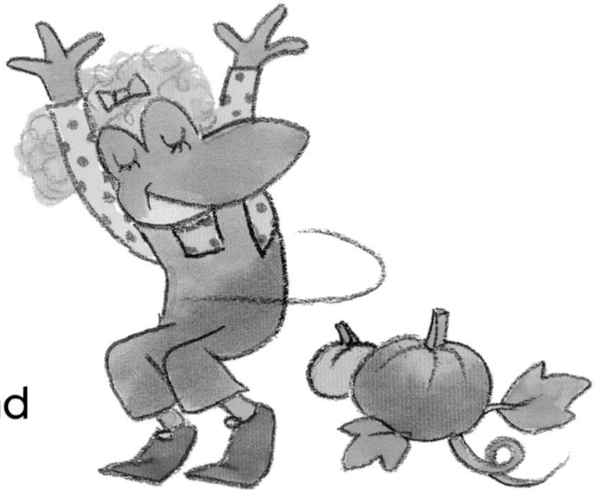

then squatted down and
said, "Hello, my sweet!"

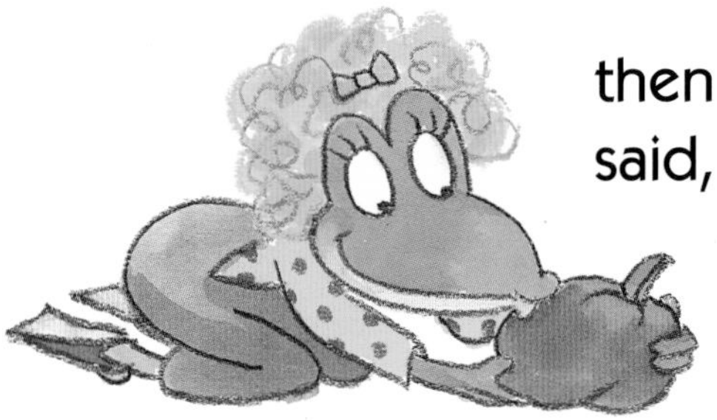

And picked up a very small,
very dark orange pumpkin,
and kissed it—*smooch!*

Froggy hopped up on
a gigantic pumpkin
and looked all around—
like a pirate on the bow of a
ship—and shouted, "Ahoy, there!"

And he leapfrogged over Frogilina.

He leapfrogged over Max.

He leapfrogged over Matthew—
flop flop . . . splat!—

and fell smack across
a *really* big pumpkin.

He stood up and said,
"This is the one!"
And he tried to pick it up.

He got it up to his knees. *Huff!*
He got it up to his chest. "YES!"

Then he trudged along
with his huge pumpkin—*lug lug UGH!*

FRROOGGYY!

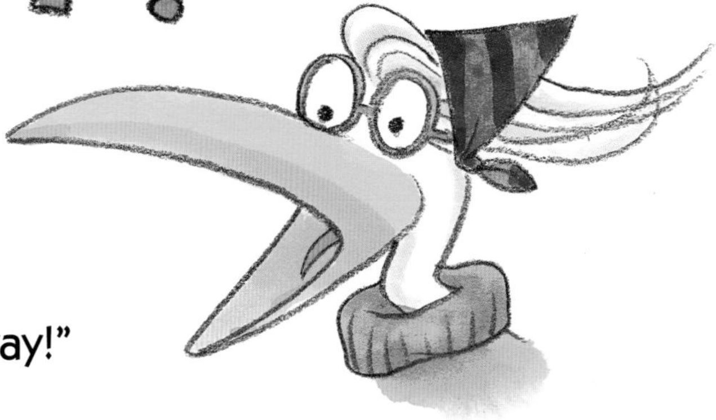

called Miss Witherspoon.
“Wha-a-a-t?”
“You’re going the wrong way!”

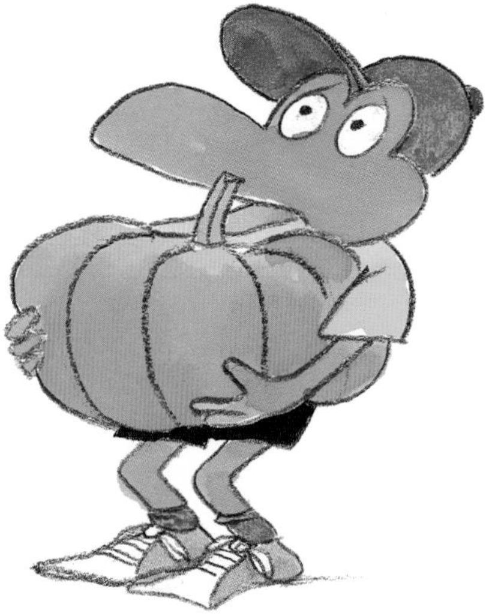

“Oops!” said Froggy,
and started huffing . . .

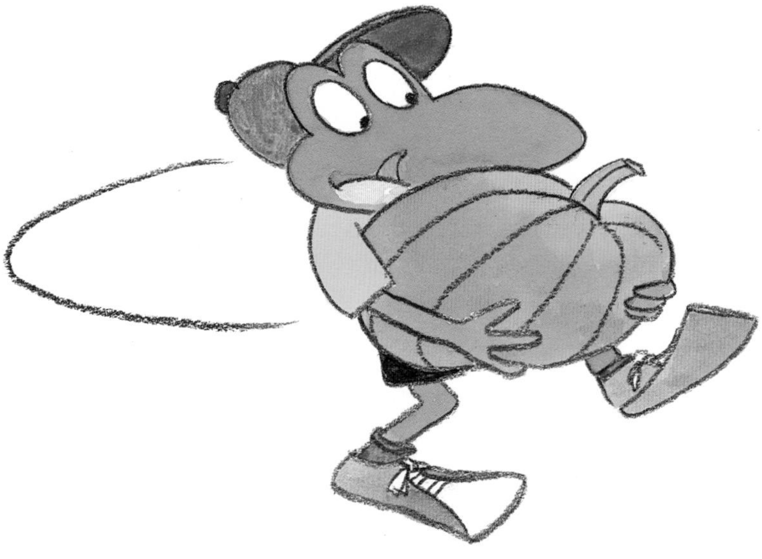

Max yelled, "Last one in is a rotten egg!"
Everybody else *ran* with their pumpkins,
and Travis rolled his big one—
rumble rumble rumble . . .

When Froggy finally got there,
he was too pooped to pop . . .
and tripped and smashed his pumpkin—
SMOOSH!

"Oops!" cried Froggy,
looking more red in
the face than green.

Everybody laughed.
Even Miss Witherspoon.

Then she said, "And now
for the winners of the
pumpkin-picking contest!

For biggest . . . Travis!

For smallest . . . Max!"
Max lifted his hat, and
there—atop his head—
was a pumpkin
the size of a golf ball.

"For prettiest . . . Matthew!
And for best all-around . . .
Frogilina!

Hers is a pie pumpkin.
Great for baking!"
Frogilina said, "Hello, my sweet!"
and kissed it—*smooch!*

Then Miss Witherspoon said,
"And for the ugliest . . .
yours, Froggy! What a mess!"
And everybody cheered,
"Hip-hip hooray!"
Even Froggy.

And on the bus ride home,
Froggy sang,
"Pumpkins, pumpkins,
muffins and pie!
Pumpkin faces lighting the sky!"
And all his friends sang with him.